Elizabeth P. Peabody

Memorial of Dr. William Wesselhöft

Anatiposi

Elizabeth P. Peabody

Memorial of Dr. William Wesselhöft

Reprint of the original.

1st Edition 2023 | ISBN: 978-3-38230-152-1

Anatiposi Verlag is an imprint of Outlook Verlagsgesellschaft mbH.

Verlag (Publisher): Outlook Verlag GmbH, Zeilweg 44, 60439 Frankfurt, Deutschland
Vertretungsberechtigt (Authorized to represent): E. Roepke, Zeilweg 44, 60439 Frankfurt, Deutschland
Druck (Print): Books on Demand GmbH, In de Tarpen 42, 22848 Norderstedt, Deutschland

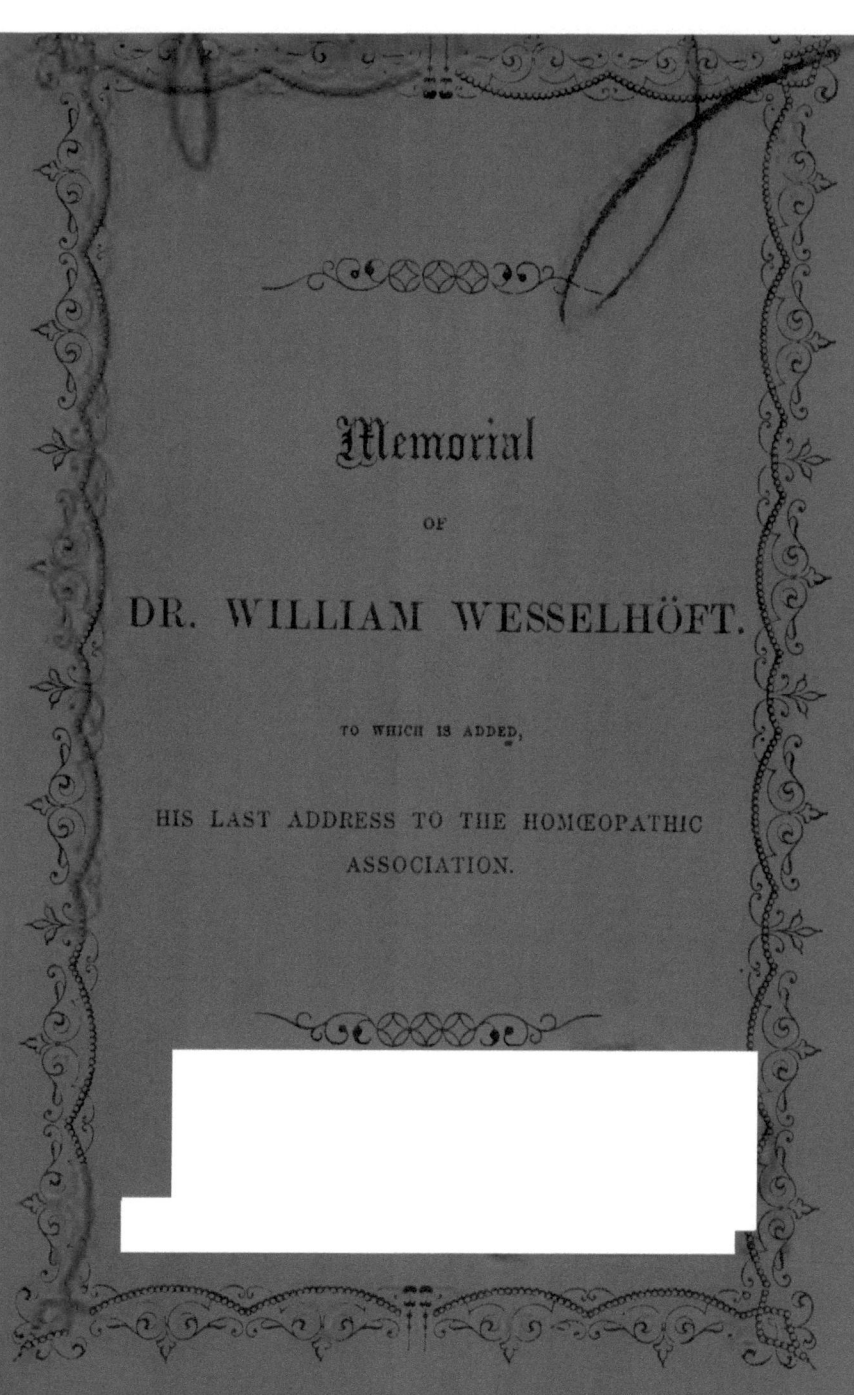

Memorial

OF

DR. WILLIAM WESSELHÖFT.

TO WHICH IS ADDED,

HIS LAST ADDRESS TO THE HOMŒOPATHIC
ASSOCIATION.

𝕸𝖊𝖒𝖔𝖗𝖎𝖆𝖑

OF

DR. WILLIAM WESSELHÖFT.

BY ELIZABETH P. PEABODY.

TO WHICH IS ADDED,

HIS LAST ADDRESS TO THE HOMŒOPATHIC
ASSOCIATION.

BOSTON:

NATHANIEL C. PEABODY,

20½, BEDFORD STREET.

1859.

MEMORIAL.

"The good die first;
While those whose hearts are dry as summer dust
Burn to the socket."

THIS has been the exclamation of Dr. Wessel-höft's friends, alternating with the word of another poet, —

"Our blessings brighten as they take the wing," —

ever since his death ; for modesty, the poetical modesty founded on the most dignified self-respect, was with him a trait so predominant, they feel that this community has "entertained an angel unawares."

And he must not pass away without some slight memorial of the sentiments with which he inspired those who knew him intimately. A few days after his death, some friends went to his afflicted family, and proposed erecting a

monument to his memory, on Forest Hill.
But it was their spontaneous and prevailing
instinct to say, "No!" It was unlike Dr. Wesselhöft to dwell in marble palaces, even in the
heyday of life. He had never any disposition
to tower among his fellows with conventional
superiorities. Every thing about him was of
intrinsic nature. A grave bursting into flowers,
with his name carved by the hands of domestic
love and personal friendship, on a low-lying
block of the mountain crystal, was in better
keeping with the spirit of his life, which, unostentatious, and rich with the life of nature,
delighted to call forth health and beauty in
others for their own sweet sake, by the opera-
tion of laws —

> "That keep the stars from wrong;
> Through which the most ancient heavens are fresh and strong."

Dr. WILLIAM WESSELHÖFT was the second
son of Karl Wesselhöft, who, with his brother-
in-law Friedrich Frommann, owned the largest
publishing-house in the university-town of Jena
during the palmy days of Saxe-Weimar. He
had moved from the town of Chemnitz when
William was four years old. Karl Wesselhöft was a man of great energy and decision,

and some severity of character : but his wife was a woman of refined temperament and intellect, of tender sensibility and disposition ; loving the beauty of nature ; forever garnering "the harvest of a quiet eye ;" and William, her darling, inherited her traits of mind and body.

Born in 1794, when all Germany was just made newly conscious of the genius of her sons, by Göthe, Schiller, and Jean Paul, it was William Wesselhöft's happy fortune to open his eyes upon life in Saxe-Weimar's richest era of science and literature. The great Göthe was a familiar guest at the house of his uncle Frommann, which was the rendezvous of the literati of Jena at that time ; and not unfrequently at his own father's house. When William was ten years old, the model student of the eighteenth century took a kindly interest in his commencing education, and gave pencils and paper and friendly counsels to him and his brother Robert (who was a year younger), in order to induce them to draw : for Göthe considered drawing an essential of early education ; and it is well known he excelled in this accomplishment himself, and pursued it to his latest days.

This was but the first omen of the beautiful culture and superior society whose advantages our friend enjoyed. Though Karl Wesselhöft, like the rest of his contemporaries, did not escape the impoverishment widely produced in Germany by the wars of Napoleon, he did not stint the education of his children. A German of the old country considers science and literature as much a necessary of life as bread, if not as breath itself.

He had, residing in his family, for private tutor of his children, the celebrated De Wette, afterwards Professor of Theology at Berlin, and later at Basle; and, after De Wette, the excellent Dr. Grossman, who died Superintendent of the Lutheran churches at Leipsic. This family school consisted of William, his brothers Edward and Robert, his sister Wilhelmina, and a ward of his uncle Frommann's, Minna Herzlieb, celebrated in the memoirs of Göthe as one of those ladies who won the great poet's heart *for a season.*

The education shared by these girls was therefore æsthetic, and a very careful one; as may be inferred from the circumstance, that Wilhelmina, when but fifteen or sixteen years of age, went for a year to the house of the

clergyman Hecker, near Leipsic, to teach his
children French and other things; and there,
as much of a playfellow as a governess, laid
the foundation of a lasting friendship with
Ferdinanda Hecker, who was at the time but
fourteen years of age, and ever afterwards
visited the Wesselhöfts at Jena, and at length
married Robert.

The correspondence with his sister, which
Dr. William Wesselhöft diligently kept up,
during all his American life, until her death
in 1844, formed a little treasury of her letters,
which, with those of his beloved mother, he
carefully preserved to re-peruse in his old age;
a period to which he looked forward in the
spirit of Robert Browning, in the hope and
intention to —

> " Retire apart
> With the hoarded memories of the heart;
> And gather all, to the very least,
> Of the fragments of life's earlier feast,
> Let fall through eagerness to find
> The crowning dainties left behind;
> Ponder on the entire past,
> Laid together thus at last,
> When the twilight helps to fuse
> The first fresh with the faded hues;
> And the outline of the whole,
> As round eve's shades their framework roll,
> Grandly fronts for once the soul."

This blessed season, alas! never came to him; but, —

  " Like the hand which ends a dream,
  Death, with the might of his sunbeam,
  Touching the flesh, the soul awoke," —

as we cannot doubt, to a fuller communion with his loved ones in the land of souls made perfect for the " communion of the just."

In 1809, William Wesselhöft became a pupil at the Real-Schule of Nuremburg, then under the direction of G. H. von Schubert, in whose autobiography is made frequent mention of this favorite pupil of the great natural philosopher and psychologist. Here, besides studying Latin and Greek, he began his profound studies in the natural sciences, including anatomy, of which he was especially fond; and he also became very expert in anatomical drawings. Throughout his life, all branches of natural history were favorite pursuits. His botanical studies were very extensive; and his choice *hortus siccus*, with written explanations of every plant, is in the possession of his wife, herself an ardent lover of flowers. During all his student-life, he was in the habit of extensive pedestrian tours to make personal explorations in botany, mineralogy, and geology. His collections of mineral and geologic specimens he very recently put into the hands of his friend, Dr. Adolphe Douai, who has undertaken to teach these sciences, among others, to the students in the Perkins Institution for the Blind, whose handling of the specimens serves all the purposes of sight.

But Dr. Wesselhöft did not confine himself to mere accumulations of phenomena in the different departments of nature. He penetrated into the principles of transcendental physics, and completed his studies with the celebrated Oken himself; with whose numerous works, among others, his library is enriched.

In 1813, being nineteen years of age, he entered the University of Jena, with high qualifications for profiting by its lectures on the Philosophy of History and other sciences: and there he graduated, seven years after, as doctor of medicine ; having perfected his general and medical education at the Universities of Berlin and Wurzburg, at each of which he resided for a season, and at which he passed the second and third examinations, necessary in Germany for obtaining a license for medical practice.

Nor did these eighteen or twenty years of

school and university education make William
Wesselhöft a mere book-worm. Never was a
scholar less pedantic in his manners. While
at Jena, he enjoyed, as has been already men-
tioned, the æsthetic society of cultivated women
as well as men, at his uncle Frommann's, who
delighted to have his gifted and cultivated nephew to adorn his re-unions with the modest
charm of his refined manners and mind.

This was the time when Göthe was so much
interested in meteorology ; and William Wesselhöft very much enjoyed making observations
on the clouds for him, at the Observatory of
Jena. He did this constantly for a year, and,
by making sketches of the clouds in water-
colors, turned to account that skill in drawing
to which his illustrious friend had given him
the first impulse in his early childhood. Göthe
afterwards gave up the notion of determining
the weather by the classification of the forms
of clouds, and laughed at it himself. But
Dr. Wesselhöft used often playfully to allude
to his having been *clerk of the weather* for a
year ; and, to his latest day, was exceedingly
fond of looking at the skies, and observing
the times and seasons and circumstances of the
strati, cumuli, schirri, &c. A pencil, which he

always cherished as a precious relic, because it was one that Göthe gave him while they were pursuing these investigations together, is preserved still among the family treasures.

But Dr. Wesselhöft was not drawn into political indifferency by his intimacy with the scientific and artistic Göthe. He gave his heart and hand, with all the ardor of youthful love, to the noble young men who had returned from fighting the battles of German nationality, in which Körner fell in 1806. When in Berlin, in 1819, he became very intimate with " the old Jahn," who invented the modern system of gymnastics, and had established in that city a gymnasium as early as 1811. In the " Memoirs of Dr. Follen," published in Boston in 1842, there is quite an extended notice of this Frederic Ludwig Jahn. He published a work upon German nationality (" Deutsches Volksthum"), whose doctrine was, by means of thorough physical education, to produce a manly character in the German youth, in the spirit of the motto which he adopted for himself and his students, " Frisch, frei, frölich, und fromm " (Strong, free, joyous, and pious). As Dr. Follen's memoirs are accessible to every-body, we will simply refer to this account, in-

stead of reproducing it. The Wesselhöfts and
Dr. Follen were intimately acquainted. The
friend referred to in his memoirs, who induced
Dr. Follen to go to Jena to lecture on the Pan-
dects, was Dr. Robert Wesselhöft, then a lawyer and holding office under the government,
and who afterwards bravely wrote a pamphlet
to defend Dr. Follen against the infamous
slanders of the " Memoirs of Herr von Döring."
From this pamphlet are given many extracts,
that not only throw great light on the noble
character and career of Dr. Follen in Germany,
but necessarily involve a vivid view of the
spirit and character of all the German students
of that era, including Jahn's scholars.

In a slight memoir of Dr. Wesselhöft that
has appeared in the " Weimarer Zeitung "
since his death, it is said that he shared, with
many of Jahn's scholars, " die Wohnung auf
der Hausvogtei, und alsbald die Gewissheit,
im Vaterland keine Anstellung zu finden."

This non-committal sentence, of the timid
conservative friend who penned that memoir,
covers facts which may be less darkly hinted
at in our free America. The Burschenschaften,
or secret political societies for promoting the
German nationality, and, in the end, uniting

Germany under one government, originated at Jena, while William Wesselhöft and his brother Robert were students; and none were more engaged and active in them than they. By correspondence, the mother-society spread its organization through all the German universities; but the branch-societies took different complexions, according to local influences. Some merely contented themselves with making a theoretical opposition to the Landmannschaften, which were aristocratic, or conservative, societies. Some went prospectively into details as to what was to be done to rid Germany of the incubus of the reigning families, who farmed it out for their own pleasure, reckless of the welfare of their subjects; and these were disposed to re-establish the republican forms which were indigenous in Germany. Many of them were inspired by Dr. Follen with the idea of a Christian republic, to be evolved from themselves as elements, by their earnest individual strivings after Christian perfection and national progress. In Dr. Follen's memoirs, to which we have already referred, are some elaborate details concerning the societies of this phase, taken partly from Robert Wesselhöft's pamphlet spoken of above;

to which we are the more willing to refer our
readers, because there can hardly be a more
profitable study for American youth than those
particular gymnastic communities which Dr.
Follen's spirit ruled.

But when, not long after, the strictly individual attempt of the rash and theory-intoxi-
cated Sand had given a bad name to the
patriots, these Burschenschaften were betrayed
to the government by a traitor; and all the
societies were confounded together in a sweep-
ing condemnation, — the Christian Follen and
his friends with Red Republicans. The discovery of the Carbonari in Italy was simulta-
neous with the discovery of the Burschenschaften in Germany; and the arrests in Germany were as unexpected and indiscriminate
as those in Italy. Thus, among others, William Wesselhöft, who was at the moment pursuing his studies in Berlin, was thrown into
the *Hausvogtei*, which is a prison for political
offenders; and Robert Wesselhöft, into the
fortress of Magdeburg. William Wesselhöft,
however, found means to escape, after a two-
months' imprisonment, and was for a long time
after concealed in his father's house at Jena.

Under these circumstances, it is not sur-

prising that the impulse developed itself within him to go and assist the struggling Greeks;
whose movement for freedom came like the
sound of a trumpet, from the old glorious
times, upon all the cultivated young men in
Europe, and even reached those of America.
It was characteristic of the generosity and
courage of William Wesselhöft, that, with his
all-sided medical education perfected, — and
which included even a knowledge of the ma-
nufacture of surgical instruments, — he should
become surgeon to the German Philhellenen,
just as the news came of the disastrous battle
of Peta, in which all the officers of the corps
of French and Germans had perished, with
two-thirds of the members. He started well
equipped with the furniture of a surgeon.
The quantities of lint scraped and bandages
oversewed by the enthusiastic sympathy of his
sister Wilhelmina, his friend Ferdinanda, and
others who were in the secret, were so ample
that they have served him for his surgery all
his life, and are not yet exhausted. For he
was disappointed of this expedition. When he
arrived at Marseilles, he found an injunction
laid upon the vessel. No more volunteers
could go to Greece.

From Marseilles, he went back to Switzerland, where already his friends Follen and Beck, — the latter a step-son of his old tutor, De Wette, — and De Wette himself, had fled; and found congenial callings at the ancient University of Basle, which was then recently re-opened. In this university, Dr. Wesselhöft also found employment as demonstrator of anatomy and assistant oculist; and he remained busily occupied in instruction two years, spending his vacations in pedestrian tours among the mountains: for not only explorations in natural science, but a pure love of the picturesque, was a great motive of his pedestrian excursions at all times. The scenery of every part of Germany that was beautiful or grand was already familiar to him by the same means; and now that of Switzerland became so, and he was never weary of the Alpine flora. During the latter years of his life, he cherished the hope and intention of revisiting these scenes in Germany and Switzerland, that "haunted him like a passion;" and when he was weary, as he often was, by the pressure of his unremitting labors, nothing soothed and beguiled him more surely than for his sons and nephews — to whom he had given a European education — to describe to him their peregrinations in those familiar scenes. The last picture that he purchased in the summer in which he died was a remarkable sketch of the Alps, painted by Leute, where the needlewood-pines seem to whisper of their solitude, and, as he said, of his "own youth."

The same interference of the allied powers with the German refugees in Switzerland, that drove Drs. Follen and Beck from Basle, compelled Dr. Wesselhöft to leave for America at the same time. Some letters which showed his sympathy with Dr. Follen had fallen into the hands of the agents of the despots. He came across the ocean, however, in a different vessel, which sailed from Antwerp, and was four months on the sea.

Exile from home and friends was a sad thing to a temperament so affectionate as Dr. Wesselhöft's; and his love of nature's beauty, no less than the generous enthusiasm he had cherished for the freedom and unity of Germany, had made the very soil of his native Europe dear. But he was still young enough to be susceptible to all the generous hopes which the ideal republican of Europe reposes in the destiny of the United States of America. He felt himself strong in the consciousness of the high cultivation of mind which makes a man the conqueror of success, wherever he may be placed. Immediately after his arrival, he went to Lehigh County, Penn., where was settled a German family which he had known at home. From thence he proceeded to Northampton County, seeking a sphere for his medical practice; and finally settled in Bath,— attracted, perhaps, by the German population.

This was not done, however, without efforts having been made by Drs. Follen and Beck to have him come to them in Massachusetts. It was in 1825 that Prof. Ticknor, at their instance, wrote to ask him to take charge of the Gymnasium at Cambridge and Boston; which they hoped would reproduce Jahn's establishment at Berlin, though it never did so. He refused, however; for already a large and profitable practice was opening upon him at Bath: and here, in the course of a few years, he married Miss Sarah Palmer, in whose family he had become intimate by his professional calls to it as an allopathic physician. Both German and English were spoken in this family; and its members had early become his warm friends.

But already he meditated the change in his practice; and as this must risk his income, at least for some years, he spoke to his wife of the plan before he married her. He represented to her that his study of medicine at the greatest medical schools of Germany — at Jena, Berlin, and Wurzburg — had still left his mind unsatisfied with any known system of therapeutics; and his practice had confirmed his doubts.

"As to therapeutics," said the lamented young James Jackson, in his frank letters to his father from the Medical School of Paris, in 1835, — after he had studied, not only in Boston, but in Edinburgh and London, — "we have not yet come within sight of its shores." So also felt the accomplished Wesselhöft ten years before the date of that letter, and for similar reasons; viz., because he was thoroughly instructed in the so-called scientific medicine of the schools, and had measured the limitations of it, and was himself thoroughly honest, and with sufficient faith in nature and God to believe, with George Herbert, that —

" All things unto our flesh are kind
In their descent and being, as to our mind
In their ascent and cause."

"Herbs gladly cure our flesh, because that they
Find their acquaintance there."

Not long after Dr. Wesselhöft had come to
America, some of the first physicians of Weimar, and many of his own most respected
classmates, had become converts to the therapeutics of Hahnemann: and the latter wrote
to Dr. Wesselhöft, urging upon him to make
trial of the medicines; which were sent him,
together with Hahnemann's organon and
" provings," by his father, who had also become a convert to the system as patient. At
first, he was averse to what seemed to be the
other absurd extreme from the then prevalent
method of giving immense doses of such medicines as calomel; the physicians of the day
vying with each other in the bold practice of
enlarging doses to the utmost extent from
which any patient could rally, and under which
numerous persons sank.

The new method asked for experiment.
Hahnemann was accustomed to say to physicians who declared to him that his new organon struck them as absurd or inconclusive,

"But try the medicines;" which was certainly Baconian philosophy. Then there was nothing absurd or even new in the principle of *similia similibus curantur*, which was an aphorism of Hippocrates. The old method had proceeded on the theory of creating artificially another disease in the sick body, because, such is the unity of the human organization, there cannot be two centres of inflammation in it at once. The new method, assuming that the cause of disease lay in the irregular action of the imponderable forces which are resumed in the word "vitality," proposed to aggravate artificially the symptom which betrayed the disorder, that the re-action might restore the equilibrium. The question between two such practical methods could never be settled, except by experiment. Dr. Wesselhöft was not converted by the organon; but he was very much struck with Hahnemann's "provings." He felt it was no more than due respect to a man, who had worked for twenty years himself, together with other men as earnest as himself, in making a materia medica, to examine it carefully. It had a quite different history, certainly, from the quack nostrums which frequently solicit the attention of the public: it had a scientific origin.

The same love of truth and independence of tradition which had inspired his studies with Schubert and Oken, together with his personal modesty on the one hand and his faith in the perfection of nature on the other, compelled him to investigation. And, when he had become convinced by personal observation that Hahnemann's preparations were effective, no timid conservatism, no considerations of material prudence, restrained him from dropping the methods he had already suspected of creating as much disease as they cured, and of adopting one against which there was, at the time, the universal prejudice which always attends new discoveries: for in science, as in spiritual life, the *opus operatum* is ever liable to become the stumbling-block, rather than the stepping-stone, of progress.

Unquestionably, the pupil of Oken, who had accepted as a principle, that the human was the metropolis of all organizations, was not wholly unprepared for a system which implies that there are occult relations between the imponderable forces that difference the various substances that compose the mineral, vegetable, and animal kingdoms, and the various organs and functions of the human body.

Dr. Wesselhöft came to believe, at last, that health and longevity were the normal state and natural right of the human race; that the healthy body would resist external causes of disease to an incalculable extent; that it was the office and duty of the medical profession, not only to discover the laws of hygiene, but to medicate "every ill that flesh is heir to," as a means of that discovery. The final object of the medical profession, he would say, is to make itself unnecessary. That universal health would be produced in the future of the human race upon earth was his entire faith; and, with the indefatigable patience that such faith works, he always labored to unfold and apply such knowledge as Hahnemann had published, and to follow in his path of carefully enlarging the *materia medica*, which he believed would at last comprehend the quintessences of the entire circle of natural substances.

The infinitesimal doses were the hardest part of the method for him to accept, though his common sense had revolted from the maximum doses of the allopathic practice. His very first experiment was in a case of ozæna, whose symptoms indicated Hahnemann's thirtieth dilution of some medicine. He said, "I was really ashamed to give the thirtieth dilution, and substituted the sixth!" When he went to his patient the next day, he found her sitting up in bed, with the symptoms immensely aggravated, and very angry. It was a lesson to him which he did not forget. The disease was cured without another dose, as it might have been with far less suffering to the patient had he given the finer dilution.

For the *rationale* of the infinitesimal dose is, that, when the right medicine is found, — the medicine which is the positive to the negative condition of the affected organ, — it is the desideratum to get the smallest degree of force to act upon it, on the principle that using a large dose is striking a sore place cruelly. The perfection of homœopathic practice is when the aggravation is so delicate, that there is no sensation of it at all; but the effect is only manifested by restoration of the body to the normal state of health. And hence it is so common for the new patients of homœopathic physicians to doubt whether it was the

medicine that cured; though it is true, that it
is rather those who are about the patients, than
the patients themselves, to have this doubt.
But there are multitudes of cases where nei-
ther patient nor observer can doubt; and these
soon multiplied in Dr. Wesselhöft's practice.
Among his first successes was his treatment of
croup with spongia and hepar. He communi-
cated these cases to the best-instructed German physicians in his neighborhood, — Dr.
Freytag, a Moravian, of Bethlehem; and Dr.
Detwiller, of Hellertown,— and engaged them
and others in the experimental investigation.
So great was the respect that Dr. Wessolhöft's
personal characteristics had inspired, that,
although some individuals were angry that he
would not administer to them at their desire
allopathic medicines, most of those who had
employed him before continued to do so, and
took the small doses: for, when he became
convinced that the homœopathic method was
true, he felt it to be the best evidence that the
allopathic method was false; and his conscience
would not permit him to tamper with this
fearful and wonderful human frame. He
used to say, that if, when it was well consti-
tuted, it was hard to drive from it the life,

even with the whole circle of poisons, it was always easy enough to fill it with chronic anguish, to be transmitted for generations. There is scarcely a drug in the allopathic practice of which Hahnemann does not note the effects as diseases, and give the antidotes. Dr. Wesselhöft tested these notations in his own practice as fast as possible, and in no instance came to a conclusion in opposition to Hahnemann's. However he might speculate, as Dr. Joslin has done (whose "Five Lectures" was a favorite book of his, which he liked to put into the hands of his patients, to show them that homœopathy might have a rational theory also), his own method was the strictly Baconian one of experiment, — observation of the phenomena, and inductions therefrom. The *art* of medicine was with him a more serious consideration than the theory; and his delicate and tender humanity secured that there never should be a careless or reckless experiment.

With views so serious and generous, it was not possible for Dr. Wesselhöft to content himself with personal success. The increasing interest in homœopathy soon suggested a Prover's Union, of which he early became a

director, and in which he was always interested.
The homœopathic practice began to spread.
Dr. Constantine Hering, who was a student
at the Medical School of the University of
Wurzburg after Dr. Wesselhöft, and had afterwards studied with Hahnemann himself, came,
in 1830, to Pennsylvania from Surinam, where
he had been practising for some years. Hear-
ing of Dr. Wesselhöft's practice, he immediately
sought him ; and they conferred upon measures
for establishing a medical school. Some highly
gifted and well-educated physicians of Philadelphia, New York, and other places, had
become converts. It is also true, and " pity
'tis, 'tis true," that a great many practitioners
sprang up all over the country, who were not
well educated in pathology or general science,
but who could take Hull's Jahr and other
works of the kind, and, by means of that tact
so very common a characteristic of Americans,
treat acute and well-defined symptoms so felici-
tously as to astonish and gain the confidence
of multitudes. Dr. Wesselhöft always said of
these practitioners, that they did not do so
much harm as even educated allopathists necessarily do ; because the medicines, if mistaken,
were generally harmless, the specifics requiring

a certain susceptibility in the patient to insure
an effect. It was chronic disease, where symptoms were obscure and complicated, that was
the test of a fully educated homœopathic physician. Still it was mortification to him, who
had the interests of the system so much at
heart, that the allopathic physicians of our
principal cities, often highly educated in general
science and accomplished in literature, should
have the chance of reproaching homœopathy
with the ignorance of its practitioners.

It is not worth while to go into the details
of the foundation of the school at Allentown.
A company was formed, and six acres of land
purchased in a beautiful spot, and the two wings
of a large building erected, where resorted
students (generally speaking, allopathic physicians who had become converts to Hahnemann's principle). Dr. Hering became the
director and chief instructor.

But the constitution of the school was never
quite satisfactory to Drs. Hering and Wesselhöft. Too many of the company had only a
pecuniary interest in its success, and were in-
clined to sacrifice the interests of the system
by admitting unqualified students.

Dr. Hering was invited into Philadelphia,

where a large practice awaited him, and where he could choose those students to whose instruction he would devote himself. Then Dr. Wesselhöft removed from Bath to Allentown, and took up the forlorn hope ; although, by so doing, he abandoned again a large and lucrative practice. It was, however, a vain attempt. He also became discouraged about the school ; and, in 1842, determined to remove to Boston, Mass., although his removal to Allentown had not proved the pecuniary disadvantage he expected it to be ; for his practice there immediately became extensive and profitable.

There was also a domestic reason for this removal. For a year before he left Allentown, he had had the happiness of the society of his brother Robert and his family. Robert Wesselhöft was, as has been said, a distinguished lawyer in Weimar, and officer of the government, when he was arrested, with other members of the Burschenschaften, and imprisoned at Magdeburg. It was not *carcere duro*, like that of the Italians in Spielburg ; but, during the seven years of his imprisonment, he had considerable intercourse, especially with the physicians of Magdeburg, and devoted himself to the study of natural sciences and medicine, and became interested in hydropathy.

Being released from prison at the accession
of Frederic William IV. of Prussia, who sig-
nalized that event by setting free all the political prisoners, he returned to Jena, where he
immediately married, resumed the practice of
his profession, and had his old office conferred
upon him again. But it was found that his
long imprisonment had not at all changed
his liberal principles, and he was the more
interesting to many by reason of his long mar-
tyrdom to them. His influence, in short, was
feared ; and the government, who could find
no pretext for making any accusation against
him, at length requested him to leave Europe,
and proposed to pay him a large sum of money
— considerably more than would cover the ex-
pense — if he would remove with his family to
America.

But, while he was yet in Europe, he had
gone to the water-cure establishments of Ilme-
nau and Carlsbad for his own health, which
had been injured by his imprisonment, and his
subsequent labors in his office ; and thus he had
become acquainted with the *practice* of water-
cure : and he came to America with quite an
enthusiasm to spread it in the New World,
where, as yet, there was not one establishment.

Dr. William Wesselhöft approved of water-cure as an agent of hygiene ; but he succeeded in convincing his brother, that it did not take the place entirely of medication by homœopathic remedies ; and Robert was initiated by his brother into the materia medica, during his year's residence in Allentown.

But Dr. William Wesselhöft gave his hearty sympathy to the project of establishing the water-cure. Water was an admirable regimen to purify the system which had been abused by drugs, and restore its normal susceptibility to the delicate medication of Hahnemann. When Dr. Robert Wesselhöft had been able, during a residence of a year or two in Cambridge, to obtain some co-operation in his plan, Dr. William Wesselhöft, who removed to Boston meanwhile, and immediately entered upon a large and lucrative practice, proved his most efficient aid in founding the Brattleborough Water Cure.

There is no doubt that Dr. Wesselhöft had the most agreeable expectations, with respect to society, in removing from the interior of Pennsylvania to Boston ; as he had not been insensible to the immense change from Saxe-Weimar to Northampton County, where, though

the population was friendly and most respecta-
ble, it left the scholar and gentleman to sigh
occasionally for the circles of his youth, which
Göthe had graced with front sublime as Jove,
and where Jean Paul Richter poured out his
rich and beautiful humor. He doubtless expected that he should find himself in a generous and noble intercourse with the scientific
physicians of Boston, who would not fail in
courteous attention to one whose culture was
nearly unparalleled, in any country, for its
scientific completeness, however they might
demur to practitioners who had no regular
education in pathology. He probably looked
forward to persuading them to faithful examination of the new system, now that there was
so favorable an opportunity for studying it
with one who had first anxiously explored
their own ground. At all events, so generous
a mind could not suppose that so serious a
subject to humanity would be dismissed with
old saws of conservatism, spiced with cavalier
jokes, without even the pretence of serious
examination. Very poor seemed to him that
kind of wit which tyrannized over the medical
society of Boston, compared with the rich
humor of his countryman and personal friend,

Jean Paul, — das Einige, — that had played, like the educating sunshine, over the morning of his own life ; and which, instead of terrifying the weak and vain and susceptible, with coxcombical sneer, from that which might perhaps be known, burst through the barriers of the dead past, and found new worlds of life to sport in, with the creative frolicsomeness of inventive power, irrepressible in its glorious courage, as the spirit of Hafiz, when he proposed to " break up the tiresome old sky."

Dr. Wesselhöft subsequently passed his own sons and nephews through the Medical School of Boston, because he was altogether too liberal to undervalue, in their own departments of science, those who took no pains to inquire into his possible knowledge, in that one " whose shores had not been approached within sight " by any of them, according to the confession of their own brightest ornament.

Besides, he wished those, whose medical education he directed, to know all that could be said for the errors which they were to oppose in their practice ; having a serious contempt for the wisdom that preserved its own self-respect by ignoring what, if admitted, might possibly show its treasures to be folly.

Dr. Wesselhöft, as Mr. Parker said at his funeral, when he saw what his path was to be, had too much dignity to complain, or rail at or ridicule others; but, with modest self-respect, proceeded to *practise down* opposition, for which he had ample opportunity.

He was not wholly alone. There were already four or five homœopathic physicians in and around Boston, recent converts from allopathy; and it was noteworthy, that the extensive and lucrative practice which some of them had previously had, took away all color of suspicion that any thing but conscientious conviction had led them to the adoption of the new method. Dr. Wesselhöft's greater age and experience in this new method naturally gave him the lead; and he was soon too much absorbed in the excessive labors which his professional calls brought upon him, to regret a social intercourse with his opponents, for which he had no time. His success in the treatment of scarlet fever opened the hearts of mothers, and forthwith introduced him into the bosom of the most conservative families; for scarlet fever had become the terror of Boston. Once established in the nurseries, his influence and practice spread. His professional income soon

became so ample, that, but for the drain upon
it to support the establishment at Brattleborough, " he would have died," as a newspaper
obituary of his death observed, " rolling in
wealth."

Nor was the Brattleborough Institution un-
successful. There were years when the re-
ceipts were $25,000. But the Wesselhöfts were
better physicians than financiers. Their dear-
est objects were other than pecuniary, in establishing the homœopathic and hydropathic
systems. They gave away as much cure as
they were paid for, always in the generous
confidence, that at last, if not at first, their
disinterested faith would be appreciated, and
open the eyes of others to what they believed
to be great humane interests.

Besides, the revolutions of 1848 made immense drafts upon their sympathies, especially
those of Dr. William Wesselhöft, whose position
in Boston made him a centre of refuge. How
many gathered about his hospitable board for
several years! A political exile himself, he
knew how to feel for the political exile, who
came here so often, without the profession or
education which secured to himself a position. Nor was it the unfortunate of his own

countrymen alone that secured his sympathy
and aid. But we must turn away from a
theme on which gratitude would delight to
dwell.

Dr. Wesselhöft, after he was in Boston, still
had students of homœopathy in such measure
as he could attend to in his private study;
but he especially interested himself in educating the young men of his own and brother's
family, to take his place by and by as strict
Hahnemannists. When he died, there were
eight times as many homœopathic physicians
in and around Boston as there were when he
came. But many of these were of what they
call the *eclectic* school, — mingling allopathic
and homœopathic methods in what he con-
ceived to be a most unphilosophical manner,
and sometimes giving allopathic doses of homœopathic medicines. He was a strict Hah-
nemannist; but he had not any conservative
bigotry. He was aware that Hahnemann had
not completed the science and art of medicine.
He accepted the progress into higher dynamization than the thirtieth (which Hahnemann
had suggested as possible, but, as he thought,
undervalued); for experiment, of the same
kind that had convinced Hahnemann of the

efficacy of the thirtieth, sanctioned the higher
ones: and he used to say, that the kind of
theoretical arguments brought against the
highest, if allowed, would condemn even the
lowest. He preferred the word " dynamization " to " dilution ; " for the efficacy was in
their dynamic force in relation to the vital
forces, which no chemistry or mechanic laws
can estimate. The power of an infinitesimal
dose was no more, but just as, inexplicable as
the power of an infinitesimal particle of light
to awaken delight in the owner of the retina
of nerves that reflects it; or, if that is dis-
eased, to inflict torture upon it. The question
always was of *the fact:* —

    " There are more things in heaven and earth, Horatio,
      Than are dreamt of in our philosophy ; " —

and these things are of daily and unques-
tionable *experience.* Dr. Wesselhöft constantly
declared, that, in this infancy of homœopathic
science, the Baconian method of experiment
and collection of phenomena must be faith-
fully followed for a long time yet, before a
scientific explanation could be hoped ; and he
had a stern feeling of disapprobation, border-
ing on contempt, at the presumptuous levity
that so easily questioned the principles and

conclusions of the conscientious and faithful
founder of the school, who did not open his
lips until he had worked twenty years.

It would not be doing justice to our friend's
solemn convictions not to say this, however
severely it may cut in some quarters.

The character of Dr. Wesselhöft has been,
perhaps, more forcibly set forth by the mere
narrative of his life, than it can be by disqui-
sition. Love of truth and beauty; a conscience of the duty of entire and manifold
culture; industry; fidelity to every opportunity of gaining new light; a manly and
generous sympathy with all social and national
development towards freedom; delicacy and
sweetness in all family relations, and to all
friends; unostentatious hospitality that was
cosmopolitan; personal habits of self-denial
and disinterestedness that seemed hardly to
have a limit; the modest charm of uncon-
sciousness which classed him with —

> " Glad hearts, without reproach or blot,
> Who do [God's] will, and know it not;" —

kindness, that, though it was habitual and
constant as the sun, had a morning freshness
about its every manifestation; and, with all
this, a simplicity, directness, and honesty in

speech, that often offended the vain and conventional: such were the traits that characterized Dr. Wesselhöft. They enriched his life; but some of them brought about his early death, which, however, as Jean Paul has beautifully said, is *the secret of nature for getting more life*.

He was not unaware, during all the last year, that he was presuming on a constitution exhausted by the unremitting labor his profession necessarily involved: and he admitted to a brother-physician, who realized this exhausted condition more than the sufferer did himself, that he ought to give up his practice, and go to Europe; for nothing less insurmountable than the ocean could divide him from his patients. But, though he was happy in the thought that his son and nephew could take up his practice, with steadfastness of fidelity to the strict homœopathic principle like his own, he was beguiled to wait a little longer, and a little longer, to attend to some patients that did not like to be given up. Thus he ran on, in the spirit of self-sacrifice, till the silver string was suddenly loosed, the golden bowl broken, and he fell.

A few weeks in the country, which it is

pleasant to remember how he enjoyed, hardly brought to himself the conviction that he was going; for he rallied in the mountain air which he sought. But a relapse, caused by an accidental cold, brought him back to the city; and he sent to Philadelphia for his friend Dr. Hering, refusing to see all others, that he might have strength to talk with him.

About twelve hours before he could expect him to arrive, probably a sudden conviction of his impending departure struck his mind. He was sitting by his wife, with her hand in his; when suddenly he brought his other hand upon it, pressed it tenderly several times, and said, " Will you go with me ? " rose up, made two or three firm steps towards the bed, and fell upon his face. On being lifted up, they saw that he was " beyond and above."

When the tidings spread through the city that he was gone, the expression of sorrow and sympathy with the bereaved was very great. It was a touching thing to see how much the respect and love felt for him was expressed in rare and beautiful flowers. A profusion of these smiles of nature, woven into exquisite garlands and wreaths and crowns, came from his friends and patients, far and near, whose greenhouses and house-plants he had never failed to dwell upon with delight when he visited them. On the day of his funeral, these sweet tributes of affection were hung about his coffin; and the Rev. Theodore Parker — a friend, and in part a patient — stood at the head of it, and made a tributary discourse to his memory, which was responded to by the tears of a large company that encircled the weeping family. Dr. Douai followed with an impassioned address to the Germans in their own language; and then Mr. Parker, in a touching prayer, thanked God for the life that had been so noble and beneficent, and implored consolation for the misfortune such a death must ever be to the surviving. The company also went to Forest Hill; and there, under a tree, in the glow of sunset, the coffin was again opened, that every friend might take a last look at the beloved features; and, the flowers being again hung round it, a strain of exquisite vocal music, from a choir of German friends who were hidden in the trees that grew over the tomb, rose and fell, and rose and fell, for ten minutes. It seemed like the song of angels who were conveying the spirit to its heavenly home.

Dr. Wesselhöft, born into the Lutheran communion, sympathized with the New ·Church, initiated by Swedenborg, more than with any other; though he did not belong to any organized society of it, and doubted whether Swedenborg himself intended his disciples should form any church more visible, than the communion of faith and charity to which all the churches of Christendom introduce sincere and loving souls.

We are permitted to add to our humble memorial the last words that he spoke in the Homœopathic Society, which the members, at the time of their delivery, asked him to give to the press.

. LAST ADDRESS

DR. WILLIAM WESSELHÖFT

TO THE

HOMŒOPATHIC SOCIETY OF BOSTON.

BEFORE proceeding, gentlemen, to the business of the day, allow me to make a few remarks.

Do you know the first words that Hahnemann exclaimed to the world? They were not, " Similia similibus;" not, " Certiorem medendi usum maluit." What, then, were they? " Aude sapere" were the words, as you will see on the titlepage of the Organon, — " Aude sapere," *dare to know.* " Young men," said Moleschot to his hearers, " dare to know, and do not dread the logical conclusions." Could Hahnemann have spoken a more significant sentence? Has not " Aude sapere" become the war-cry of the nineteenth century? It booms from the depth of the people's heart. The halo of earthly gods has

vanished, and their temples tumble to the
ground. The world *will know*, and strives to
become conscious ; the humblest of the people
asks, *Why?*

But is it hazardous " to know " ? *Yes, it is.*
History shows us but one continued struggle
against and persecution of truth. With perfect
right one may say, there is nothing more terrible than great truths. Pass over in your
minds the history of mankind. The first de-
sertion from absolutism * cost the German
nation alone twenty millions of human lives,
— three-quarters of the entire population ;
the most terrible fact in history. But we
must not reproach truth for this. Knowledge
itself has never injured. Blind belief was the
black ship, driven about by the storm of fana-
ticism upon an ocean of blood.

Want of firmness, on the part of the representatives of truth, was ever the greatest enemy
to truth. Even the contemporaries of Luther
had to call out to their master, " Aude sapere," — the same Luther who had dared to
brave a whole world of night and darkness ;
for Luther was still a priest. The consciousness of human rights, deeply engraved in every

---
* The Thirty Years' War.

heart, was in Luther's breast crushed by the weight of petrified dogmas; and this priestly narrowness had to be paid for by a nation's best blood. In the history of homœopathy, in the history of our own conversion, we find something analogous.

The way had already been broken for *similia similibus*: the world had already a presentiment of it. It had, here and there, been gossiped about. There were conjectures without proof. Had Hahnemann proclaimed homœopathy in scruples and grains, it would, by this time, have conquered the whole world. *Similia similibus* was not the stumbling-block; but the discovery of *the dynamization of medicinal matter* was the unheard-of thing that had never before entered a human mind.

How did we take it up? Facts, strengthened by our own repeated experiments, tumbled our entire structure of thought to the ground. There we stood, struck dumb with astonishment. We could not turn back: the road was blockaded by an overwhelming fact. This fact had to be understood; i.e., its coincidence with other facts was to be established. It was a fact, that, in the eyes of the world, branded him as crazy who stood up for it.

One grain of medical matter expanded, in a certain manner, to the magnitude of a sphere much larger than the probable diameter of our solar system, and, brought in contact through its minutest surface with the human nerves, produces, under certain conditions, the most wonderful effects.

"If that is not madness, then there is no madness!" So exclaimed the world, and we re-iterated. We heard men vow that they would disclaim all hope of salvation, if that were truth. Common sense was invoked to arouse itself. Power was called upon to suppress such madness.

Nevertheless, it was truth; and how many more such secrets may Nature have in store for us? *

---

* Science has already accepted analogous facts. The late Professor Farrar asserted, that such was the velocity of light, that to produce the fact of vision, it was not necessary for the particles to be nearer to each other than the breadth of the solar system; and that " they were so frightfully small, that had they been placed in contact on a line during six thousand years, one every second, the line would not yet have become visible to the naked eye by its *size*."

And if those, who do not believe in the atomistic theory of light, will consider, on their own theory, the fact, that stars, so distant as to be immeasurable by the human understanding, yet are patent to the eye of the most uninstructed clown, a breadth of relation of the human nerve with nature is proved, that brings homœopathic infinitesimals into the region of the common sense.

E. P. P.

At first, the higher dynamizations were widely opposed, and many homœopaths condemned them. But the Russian Korsakoff, in whose ears ever resounded the " Aude sapere ! " potentized on, higher and higher, and sent abroad his preparations for others to try the experiments; and the result was astonishing, though not quite decisive. There were sometimes great results, and sometimes none at all : this arose from the false ideas regarding these preparations, and consequent misapplication. About ten years later, Jenichen and Gross proclaimed the high potencies, with exact directions for their application ; and the result was striking. While one party went into this apparent extreme, the other submitted to it so far as to tolerate the thirtieth potency of Hahnemann; without, however, recommending that. Were it of any use to potentize farther, the existence of the thirtieth dynamization might be permitted ; while every thing over and above that was pure nonsense, against which all must be guarded, in order not to " tip out the child with the bath."

The atomistic views could be made to agree with the third dynamization ; farther than that they suffer shipwreck ; while on the highest potencies, now so much used, they go to the bottom, " man and mouse."

But, after all, by dynamization we have gained for science but one more imponderable. It astonishes us only by its newness, and by its immense relations with human welfare and medical science. Magnetism, electricity, galvanism, mesmerism, and these dynamized solids, are equally wonderful, — one not more than another. All great agencies of nature are of like fineness and penetrability.

Similia similibus does not refer only to the similarity of the medicinal symptoms with those of the disease : it also has a bearing on the similarity of all the other relations of contagious miasmata with the curative powers. 1. The sickening potencies of contagious miasmata are imponderables as well as the curative. 2. The finer and more dynamical their qualities are, so much stronger and quicker their effects. Syphilis and psora require contact for their transmittance ; but they will not prove mortal for many years : while typhus or varioloids are contagious at a great distance, and endanger life in a few days. 3. As contagious or miasmatic matter adheres with incredible tenacity to paper, wool, or other indifferent substances, so that it will last for years, and can be transferred to a great distance; in like manner do our medicinal dynamizations adhere to indifferent matter; and in this form, enclosed in little papers, they may be sent thousands of miles without losing their curative qualities. We trust to globules prepared (by trustworthy hands) twenty years ago, but place no confidence in tinctures of the same age. The mode in which Jenichen came to the high potencies seems to corroborate this opinion. It is known that Jenichen found the medicine he intended to use dried up. The vial was empty and dry. He filled it with alcohol, and was astonished at obtaining a dilution of exceedingly powerful curative properties. The medicinal power adheres to the surface of a vial similar to electricity, and is again absorbed by the fluid subsequently poured in. The dog, who smells out a trail, furnishes a phenomenon that falls within the limits of these observations. The vital sphere of an organism communicates something to the places it passes, that for a longer or shorter time will resist rain, the heat of summer, and the cold of winter, and which still may be perceived. A vial of musk may be broken in the midst of a forest; and, years afterwards, the odor can be distinctly perceived. I have in my possession a book, which, thirty-eight years ago, stood in the room of a young physician, who, in his last hours of life, had had musk prescribed to him. This book, which long ago crossed the ocean, bears the odor of musk very perceptibly to this day, especially in damp weather.

The medicinal effect of high potencies is an established fact. To him who demands more than good authority, while he does not experiment, and ask Nature herself, Hahnemann exclaims in vain, "Aude sapere!" When Mesmer came forward with his great discovery, we had a similar spectacle; and, notwithstanding the facts that have accumulated to demonstrate mesmeric power, there is a stubborn stolidity that will not bend its neck under the yoke of fact. Another benefactor of mankind in our field — Priesnitz — also had a hard battle to fight.

To know, one must have courage to stand by his knowledge. In a century from this time, men will, perhaps, occupy the same position in regard to the so-called sympathetic

cures that they now hold in regard to homœopathy. Let us keep our senses open for facts.
But, gentlemen, our aim is not only to cure
disease, but rather to prevent it. *The art of
awakening and increasing the vitality of the
human body,*—THAT is our highest aim. To
the physician, then, the highest task is given,
because soundness of mind depends so much
on a healthy body. Some virtues and powers
may even be developed in disease; but only a
healthy human being will make full use of
existence and life, and of the blessings of science and art in the production of the highest
results.

As boys, we are led up to a past world of
vigor and beauty. Our hearts tremble, and
our eyes beam; but notwithstanding all the
science, all the great discoveries and inven-
tions, we boast, and of which antiquity is void,
we remain physically wretched. " There's
something rotten in the state of Denmark;"
or, to use Schiller's words, "A dismal spirit
steals through our house." Whence the general want of a grand evolution of mind?
Where is the impediment that makes this
Christian life so full of effeminate morality?
Here let " Aude sapere " thunder in our ears,

and lead us to the discovery of some perfect
everlasting truth, that, like *similia similibus*,
will morally compel us to follow a logical
train of thought, and boldly to meet the con-
sequences eye to eye.

Much might be said on this subject; but
only one thing I will name here, be it cause
or effect. *Our physical education is wretched,
and unworthy of a great and free nation.*
Charles Follen strove, in the service of humanity, to mend these deficiencies by trying
to introduce gymnastics as an essential branch
of the total system of education; but the time
for this had not arrived. In Germany, endeavors of this kind have been more frequent,
and received with more sympathy; though
tyranny has there stifled these infant Hercules
in their cradles. The institutions called "children's gardens" drew forth all delicate children
of one neighborhood from the body-and-soul-
killing four walls of city dwellings into the
open air, where they became impressed with
the beauties of nature; where they learned
to express themselves in words, and thus received the first rudiments of a republican life.
For the age of advanced boyhood, the gymnastic school of Jahn was created. What was

seen and experienced there will ever be remembered. A better future beamed from every eye, germinated in every body. A shadow of this life has maintained itself among the Germans in America; and it is the only grand bond of union still existing in this race, so prone to separation and disunion.

Gentlemen, laxatives and tea are two great representatives of what has depressed the generations: gymnastics and homœopathy will elevate them again. If I had only the choice between the introduction of homœopathy on the one hand, and that of gymnastics and physical education on the other, I would resort to the latter, notwithstanding that Hahnemann is my guide through the labyrinth of dyscrasic diseases; for, without physical education, the physician's activity would for ever remain confined to the limits of the cobbler's bench. Through physical education and gymnastics, we must form a soil in the human body on which a dyscrasy cannot continue to flourish; and that which is not allowed to advance will go backwards. Such a thing as standing still between progression and retrogression does not exist in nature. Through endeavors prolonged through several generations for the healthy development of the human body, health and beauty would return to the earth.